# Note to parents, carers and teachers

*Read it yourself* is a series of modern stories, favourite characters and traditional tales written in a simple way for children who are learning to read. The books can be read independently or as part of a guided reading session.

Each book is carefully structured to include many high-frequency words vital for first reading. The sentences on each page are supported closely by pictures to help with understanding, and to offer lively details to talk about.

The books are graded into four levels that progressively introduce wider vocabulary and longer stories as a reader's ability and confidence grows.

## Ideas for use

- Begin by looking through the book and talking about the pictures. Has your child heard this story before?

- Help your child with any words he does not know, either by helping him to sound them out or supplying them yourself.

- Developing readers can be concentrating so hard on the words that they sometimes don't fully grasp the meaning of what they're reading. Answering the puzzle questions at the end of the book will help with understanding.

*For more information and advice on Read it yourself and book banding, visit* **www.ladybird.com/readityourself**

Book Band
5

**Level 1** is ideal for children who have received some initial reading instruction. Each story is told very simply, using a small number of frequently repeated words.

## Special features:

Opening pages introduce key story words

Large, clear type

Jon liked to play football.
Ollie and Jess liked to play football, too.

Careful match between story and pictures

## Educational Consultant: Geraldine Taylor
## Book Banding Consultant: Kate Ruttle

LADYBIRD BOOKS

UK | USA | Canada | Ireland | Australia
India | New Zealand | South Africa

Ladybird Books is part of the Penguin Random House group of companies
whose addresses can be found at global.penguinrandomhouse.com.

ladybird.com

Penguin
Random House
UK

First published 2015
001

Printed in China

A CIP catalogue record for this book is available from the British Library

ISBN: 978-0-723-29517-4

# Jon's Football Team

Written by Ronne Randall
Illustrated by Charlie Alder

team

Jon

Ollie

football

goal

Jess

Ben Wills

7

Jon liked to play football.

Ollie and Jess liked to play football, too.

9

Jon, Ollie and Jess played with a team.

All the mums and dads came to see the team play.

Jon's team had a match with some big boys and girls. They did not score goals.

The other team scored all the goals!

The other team won the match. The big boys and girls were happy.

Jon and his team were not happy.

Jon and his dad went to see a big football match. Jon's team went, too.

Ben Wills scored all the goals.

Jon and his team liked
Ben Wills.

"We can play football like
Ben Wills," said Jess. "We can
score goals like he did!"

Jon's team had a match with the big boys and girls.

Jess kicked the ball to Ollie.

"Good kick!" said a man.

21

Ollie kicked the ball to Jon.

"Good kick!" said the man.

Jon kicked the ball.

"Good kick!" said the man.

Jon scored a goal!

Jon's team won the match!

They were very happy.

Some mums and dads
came over.

"Good match!" they said.

The man came over, too.
The man was Ben Wills!

"Good match, team," said Ben Wills. "Good goal, Jon!" he said.

Jon was very, very happy!

How much do you remember about the story of Jon's Football Team? Answer these questions and find out!

- Who beats Jon's team when they play football?

- Who do Jon and his team want to play football like?

- Who scores the goal to beat the big boys and girls?

# Look at the pictures from the story and say the order they should go in.

A

B

D

# Tick the books you've read!

## Level 1

Astronauts □
Dinosaurs □
Jon's Football Team □
Fun at the Fair □
The Emperor's New Clothes □
The Enormous Turnip □
Fairy Friends □
ISLAND ADVENTURE □
Daddy Pig's Old Chair □

Goldilocks and the Three Bears □
Little Red Hen □
The Magic Porridge Pot □
Little Creatures □
Recycling Fun! □
The Princess and the Pea □
Cinderella □
The Bravest Fox □
Topsy + Tim At the Farm □

Rex the Big Dinosaur □
The Tale of Peter Rabbit □
The Three Billy Goats Gruff □
Why Giraffe has a Long Neck □
Topsy + Tim Go to the Zoo □
The Ugly Duckling □
THE RADISH ROBBER □

## Level 2

Big Machines □
Camping Trip □
THE ANGRY OWL □
Beauty and the Beast □
Chicken Licken □
The Monster Next Door □
The Gingerbread Man □
Wild Animals □
School Bus Trip □

Little Red Riding Hood □
Nature Trail □
Sports Day □
Pirate School □
Rumpelstiltskin □
Sleeping Beauty □
Dom's Dragon □
Superhero Max □
TREEHOUSE RESCUE □

Sly Fox and Red Hen □
The Tale of Jemima Puddle-Duck □
The Three Little Pigs □
Why Lion ROARRRS! □
The Big Race □
Town Mouse Country Mouse □
Topsy + Tim Go to London □

The Read it yourself with Ladybird app is now available